This book belongs to:

WITHDRAWN

who is loving, learning & growing every day!

This book is dedicated to anyone who has
ever wondered what it takes to grow great!
Bloom into your greatest self!

Copyright © 2022 by Mechal Renee Roe

All rights reserved. Published in the United States by Doubleday,
an imprint of Random House Children's Books, a division of Penguin Random House LLC, New York.

Doubleday and the colophon are registered trademarks of Penguin Random House LLC.
HAPPY HAIR is a registered trademark of Happy Hair.

Visit us on the Web! rhcbooks.com

Educators and librarians, for a variety of teaching tools, visit us at
RHTeachersLibrarians.com

Library of Congress Cataloging-in-Publication Data
Name: Roe, Mechal Renee, author, illustrator.
Title: I'm growing great / written and illustrated by Mechal Renee Roe.
Description: First edition. | New York : Doubleday Books for Young Readers, [2022] |
Audience: Ages 2–8.
Summary: "Girls' growth and positivity are celebrated in this
garden-themed inspirational book." —Provided by publisher.
Identifiers: LCCN 2021020908 (print) | LCCN 2021020909 (ebook) |
ISBN 978-0-593-42890-0 (hardcover) | ISBN 978-0-593-42891-7 (library binding) |
ISBN 978-0-593-42892-4 (ebook)
Subjects: CYAC: Stories in rhyme. | Growth—Fiction. | Gardens—Fiction.
Classification: LCC PZ8.3.R6185 Im 2022 (print) |
LCC PZ8.3.R6185 (ebook) | DDC [E]—dc23

MANUFACTURED IN CHINA
10 9 8 7 6 5 4 3 2 1
First Edition

A HAPPY HAIR® BOOK

I'M GROWING GREAT

Written & illustrated by MECHAL RENEE ROE

Doubleday Books
for Young Readers

LOVELY AND WISE, SHINE AT SUNRISE!

i am growing each day!

PLANT THE SEEDS, CLEAR THE WEEDS!

i am growing each day!

GARDEN WITH LOVE!
RISE HIGH ABOVE!

i am growing each day!

REMEMBER MY NAME!
NOTHING STAYS THE SAME!

i am growing each day!

STRETCHING MY WINGS!
HEAR MY HEART SING!

i am growing each day!

TOUGH AS A ROSE, FROM MY HEAD TO MY TOES!

i am growing each day!

TRUE TO YOU, SWEET AS MORNING DEW!

i am growing each day!

RAINY SHOWERS UNLEASH HIDDEN POWERS!

i am growing each day!

EXPLORING MY FEELINGS BRINGS KIND HEALING!

i am growing each day!

STEADY AS A TREE!
PEACE WITHIN ME!

i am growing each day!

BUILD LIKE A BEE!
PATIENCE IS KEY!

i am growing each day!

GIVE ME SOME ROOM! I'M READY TO BLOOM!

i am growing each day!

I AM BORN TO BE GREAT!